It Happens Only in Love

Amit Singh

Invincible Publishers

First published in India in 2017 by Invincible Publishers

ISBN: 978-93-86148-93-3

Invincible Publishers
G-120, Sushant Lok III, Sector 57, Gurgaon-122001

Opposite Kasturba Ashram, Radaur Distt Yamuna Nagar, Haryana- 135133
Digitally Printed at Replika Press Pvt. Ltd.

Dedicated to
All the lovely women in the world

Acknowledgement

❄ ❄ ❄

I would like to thank 'Team Invincible Publishers' led by Mr. Ajay Setia, for their co-operation and guidance throughout the process. I would also like to thank my editor, Bhavna Sharma for completing the task of fixing the language and correcting grammar errors in the script.

I would like to thank my mother sincerely, for the support she gave me without a notable gesture.

I would like to recognize my best friend Arpan Gosh for being the kind of person he is. Also, I extend my gratitude to Anita Davagotra for being my first reader, Ashutosh, Arun, Amit, Mukesh and all my friends who inspired me every day, some or the other way.

Prologue

* * *

To be successful, you need to have a clear vision and a disciplined life. Having a clear vision helps to realize the dreams of success.

But,

What if you are living a life without any vision and flowing with the time?

What if people around you move ahead and leave you behind?

What if you start realizing you are a failure?

What if you lose all hopes, get into depression and have suicidal instincts?

In both these scenarios, we need someone to hold our hand and to help us to realize our strength.

As they say, there is always a woman behind every successful man. She may be your mother, who loves you unconditionally; or she may be your sister, who fights with you for all the silly things but still supports you; or she may be your lover, who still believes in you and gives you strength to fight all the odds. You are lucky if you have someone in your life who supports and motivates you.

"It happens only in Love" is an inspiring story of love, laugh and success. An unusual Love story of Aditya and Ananya. It helps us to value of a woman's love and care in a man's life.

Chapter 1–
My Life

* * *

New Delhi

My name is Aditya, but people call me Adi. I am the most spoiled and naughtiest boy in my college as well my housing society.

Students go to college to build their career, but I go there to have fun. Bunking lectures, boys gang and dominating over other students, have arguments with security guards etc. are the things that I usually do every day in college, except studies. You call out my name in front of any teacher, student or support staff, rest is history.

My parents think that I am out of their control because according to them neither I am good in studies nor in sports.

However, I think I am a lucky boy as my name starts with the letter 'A'. I am the only loving son of my mother, Alka, and my father, Anand. My father is a retired government officer. We live in Government Quarters in R.K.Puram. My gang of childhood best friends includes Abhilasha, Abhimanyu and Ajay.

****

Being a single child doesn't always give you all the benefits as your parents have high expectations from you alone. Despite being the only apple of their eyes, you still have to prove yourself.

There are many advantages though. You are the only one who is adorable to your parents. You do not have to share your room, computer or anything with anyone. Everything belongs to you.

In my case, my parents love me a lot, but they have many expectations from me, which I have never been able to fulfill.

My mother loves me more than my father does. She has always saved me by hiding my mistakes from my father. I am very afraid of my father. His expressions used to make me cry when I was a kid. My father had always been strict with me whenever he found me guilty. I knew that whatever he did was only for my good, but I, somehow, didn't like it.

Chapter 2–
The Result Day

* * *

At Home: 28th July' 2014

Finally, the day arrived when my final year results got declared. My dad was confident that I wouldn't pass this year, considering my previous records. It took me three long years to pass my higher secondary and I could clear my senior secondary only with grace marks.

I never had keen interest in studies nor am I good at it. However, yes, I have always been an active part of several incidents, which landed people into trouble.

Therefore, my father was right that I could hardly clear my exams. But, he didn't know the secret behind my success. Abhilasha, yes, she is the secret. I have full confidence that I will clear the exams because I copied from her answer sheets and she is a brilliant student. So, my results depend upon Abhilasha's preparation.

We had discussed last night that Abhimanyu would pick all of us and we would go together to college. It was one of the toughest nights of my life. I had never been that tense throughout my school and college days. Final year results did not bother me, but the thought that what would I do after college without my friends did.

At 8 o'clock sharp, my phone rang. I disconnected the call even without checking the caller's name. I hardly slept at night and fell asleep early morning. My phone rang continuously, but I was in deep sleep.

I felt cold sensation inside my t-shirt and woke up immediately. I saw a few faces laughing at me. I rubbed my eyes and realized that my friends were standing around my bed. Ajay put ice-cubes in my t-shirt as Abhilasha pointed at him. For the next few minutes, we laughed uncontrollably.

"Hello Adi, good morning beta," Abhilasha said.

"Good morning," I replied.

"Hey dude you are still sleeping. It is 8 o'clock. Hurry and get up, we have to leave," Abhimanyu shouted.

"Just wait for 10 minutes," I replied to him and rushed towards the washroom.

In the next 15-20 minutes, we left for college in Abhimanyu's car.

While we covered the distance between my home and college, my heartbeat kept pacing up. I was numb while my friends were laughing and enjoying. I started thinking about my life after college and my future. Suddenly the car stopped and I came out of my thoughts that had occupied my mind since last night. We reached college. There was a huge rush.

****

Ramjas College, North Campus
New Delhi

It was Abhilasha, who was super excited to know the results. I was not expecting much, but just pass marks would be great. I was wishing for Abhilasha's good score because my score too depended on her scorecard. Abhilasha and Abhimanyu walked towards the notice board to check the results. While Ajay and I waited for them in the car, we were praying for our success.

It was 10 o'clock in the morning and the next few hours would decide our destiny. Students gathered all over the college campus. A few seemed very happy and the other faces looked a little upset.

I had a mixed feeling. It was more than an hour and we were still waiting for Abhilasha and Abhimanyu. During this time, Ajay and I kept quiet and did not initiate any conversation. I, then dialed Abhilasha's mobile number, but didn't get any response from her side. It was difficult to spot them in the mad crowd. Then, I saw Abhimanyu talking on phone and they both were walking towards us. Their expressions were blank. They were neither happy nor sad. They got in the car and were silent. I could not resist and after a couple of minutes, I asked about the results.

"What is the result," I asked.

"Nothing," Abhilasha replied with an expressionless look. Her reaction induced the curiosity in me.

"Hey Abhilasha, please tell us about the result."

"Ask Abhimanyu," she replied again, there was suspense.

Her reaction broke my heart and I thought to myself that my fear was real and I clearly had not passed the exams.

"Guys I feel sorry to declare that we are...," Abhimanyu muttered.

"Abhimanyu please let us know the results," Ajay requested.

"We are no more a part of Ramjas College as we all are graduates now."

His words gave me a kind of relief that is hard to explain in words. I jumped out of excitement. I thought that finally my father's opinion about me would change.

It was I, who shouted the first.

"Hip Hip Hurray"

In addition, later they joined me.

"Hip Hip Hurray"

"Hip Hip Hurray"

"Hip Hip Hurray"

That is how my gang and I celebrated the success.

"Why you guys were acting so insane," I asked Abhilasha and Abhimanyu.

"It was Abhilasha's plan," Abhimanyu replied.

"I just wanted to give you guys goose bumps and I succeeded in my plan," said Abhilasha.

"So guys the party begins," we shouted together. We screamed, and laughed and cried as well.

Chapter 3
Pyjama Party

* * *

We decided to celebrate our success at Abhilasha's terrace garden, as it was spacious. It was a theme party and we decided to wear red pyjamas with white t-shirts. As per our plan, we gathered at Abhilasha's house at 8 pm.

Sky was clear and the stars were twinkling to add shine to our party.

Ajay arranged for the wine bottles. Abhilasha cooked delicious food and I arranged for the music system and the dance floor. Abhimanyu helped us manage everything.

The party started with three cheers. We shouted as loud as we could and shook our legs on the dance floor.

Ajay served us the drinks. It was more than an hour and we were dancing and boozing.

I was tired and left the dance floor to take some rest. Abhilasha joined me.

"Thank you Abhilasha," I said.

"Thank you for what?" she asked.

"Thank you for helping me in my exams. It would not have been possible without you," I told her.

She laughed and smirked at me.

"I am not joking. Seriously, thank you for helping me pass my exams," I said.

"Adi you are mad. There is no space for thank you and sorry in friendship," she said.

Music brought about an aura of freshness, showing us the path of our career, which was waiting for us, between all this we were all relaxed to have graduated. We then enjoyed our dinner. It was pure

Indian homemade food.

"Thank you Abhilasha for such a tasty treat," said Ajay.

"Actually, this awesome food is cooked by my mother. Please give thanks to her," she replied.

"Thank you aunty," we all said together.

We were all heavily drunk and it was apparent from our speech.

Abhimanyu played some melodious songs on his guitar. We then wrapped up the party at 4 am.

Chapter 4–
Inner voice

* * *

I felt like a free bird. I had no burden of books, lectures and most importantly exams. However, the sad part was that we all had to go our way because of our future course of career.

Abhimanyu and Abhilasha went to the U.S. to study MBA after clearing GRE exams. Ajay started working with his father and assisted in his transport business.

What was I doing. I really had no idea.

I missed my friends badly. I missed the time spent with them, my college days, bunking lectures and the fun that we all used to have together. I missed everything.

I started getting bored at home. Sometimes I thought of pursuing higher studies, but my capabilities restricted me. Even my father will not spend much on me.

My friends were all busy in their lives. They pursued what they had planned, but I never really thought about my life neither was I serious about it.

I spent all my day and night in my bedroom. Gradually, over thinking pushed me into depression.

Three Months Later

One day my father called me and threw some random questions at me.

"Why are you wasting your time?"

"Why are you not thinking about your future?"

"What do you want to do in your life?"

At that time, I was all-blank. I didn't have

anything to answer to my father.

"Dad, I just want to be happy and enjoy my life," I then finally concluded.

"But, who will pay for your enjoyment. Everything comes with a price tag. You need to ask these questions to yourself. What price are you willing to pay," he shouted and left the room angrily by shutting the door behind.

That question got stuck in my head. I never thought about it.

The conversation with my dad made me realize that life was not as easy as it was portrayed in Bollywood movies. I have to fight to survive it.

******

A serious conversation with my father transformed my thoughts and compelled me to think about my life differently, about which I had never thought before. For me, life was all about having fun with friends. However, sometimes, you just have to accept that certain things cannot remain the same. I decided to find a job for myself. I prepared a resume and started searching jobs. It was for the first time that I had searched job portals. I registered my details and started preparing for interviews.

It was late night and for a boy like me it was not easy to change habits. Despite, I was now quite serious about my future, but it was not easy for me to quit surfing on social networking sites and watching porn.

One night, I was busy watching porn on my

laptop. It was two at night. Suddenly, my dad walked inside my room. I didn't realize as I was using my headphones.

"What are you doing late at night," he shouted.

When I realized his presence, I immediately put off my headphones and shutdown my laptop.

"Dad you are here." I fumbled.

"So what you have planned?" he asked.

"I am looking for jobs."

"I know how sincere you are and what are you doing at night. You must be watching nonsense things and wasting your time," he said angrily and left the room.

Chapter 5–
The Crush

❄ ❄ ❄

I used go to bed late at night and woke up late in the morning. This was my routine. My dad didn't like my habit since college days. He always poked me for my schedule. I never imagined that life would be tough after college. It would have been better if I had not cleared the exams and would have remained in the same college. Life seems so scary once you move out of college life.

However, I can't go back and rewrite my story again. Instead, I have to focus on my career to have a successful life ahead. My dad's harsh words always forced me to do something I never did before. I was missing my friends, who always made me smile whenever I was upset. I was in touch with them through either Whatsapp or Facebook.

******

One night, I was watching TV and switching channels from one to another. Random thoughts were going on in my head.

My eyes were stuck on a news channel. I stopped switching the channels. It was not the breaking news that kept me awake, but the news anchor, whose beauty mesmerized me. She looked like an angel. She was beautiful.

"Is it love at first sight?" I asked myself.

I have heard about it, watched in the movies and read it in novels as well but I didn't know what it was like really, until I experienced it.

My heart wanted to see her again. My efforts were fruitful as I found some of her videos on YouTube.

Every time I looked at her, I fell more for her and my heart skipped a beat.

******

My dad knocked the door in the middle of the night and asked the same question.

"What are you doing?"

"Dad, Dad...," I fumbled again.

"I am looking for jobs on a few job sites and forwarding my resume," I replied.

"Don't lie to me," he shouted.

"I told you many times and I am reminding you again that, be sincere with your life, else it will be too late," he explained.

"It's never too late dad, I will do something," I murmured.

I felt so relaxed when he left the room, but internally I felt bad that he was sad because of me.

Within a few minutes of regret, I forgot everything and started searching more about the girl who made me fell for her.

After a few hours of Google search and I found all about her.

Her name was Ananya Sen. Her date of birth was December 29, 1991. She was from Kolkata and lived in New Delhi. She worked as a new reader with Xpress News. What made me more relaxed was that her marital status was single.

That made me crazier about her. I forgot my pain when I thought about her.

Chapter 6–
Fake Interview

❄ ❄ ❄

The next morning was not ordinary. I woke up early despite sleeping late at night. I felt something different that I never felt before and I was smiling for no reason.

"Was this love that my heart felt for someone, who doesn't even know me," he thought to himself.

As soon as I got up from my bed, the first thing that I did was to switch on the T.V. and tuned to Xpress News. I was never interested in watching news channels, but my eyes kept looking at the 34" T.V. screen.

Half day passed and I was still watching T.V., but did not see her in the news channel. This made me sad. I had no control over my emotions. I wanted to see her. After being disappointed on my own, I decided to visit her office.

I found her office address on Google. It was in Noida, Sector 85. After my college results, it was the first time that I was stepping out of my colony.

But, I had no money as dad stopped giving me pocket money after college and I too did not ask for money.

I came out of my shell.

Dad was reading a newspaper in the drawing room.

"Hi Dad," I greeted him.

His looked at me surprisingly. In addition, why not, after all he saw me out of my room and I looked well dressed.

"Oh! What happened today and where are you going?" He questioned.

"Dad, I told you that I was preparing for some job interviews and today I have an interview scheduled," I said.

"I knew I was lying, but some lies are good if they are meant for a good reason," I thought to myself.

He smiled back at me and wished me luck.

I was still standing there.

"Do you need anything?" he asked.

"Dad, I need 500 rupees and your scooter," I requested.

He gave me the money without asking a single question as he used to do while I was in college and handed over me the keys of his Bajaj scooter.

As soon as I walked out, he called me again.

"You did not tell me in which company you are going for an interview?" he asked.

"Where is it?" he further questioned.

He asked a few rapid questions and I was not prepared to answer those.

"The company's name is Xpress News, Noida Sector-85 for the position of marketing executive," I replied.

"But it's already 4 pm and most corporate offices are closed by 6 pm. It will take an hour to reach Noida. Did you check with them," he asked.

This time he asked a tough question.

But, I still managed to reply him.

"Actually, it is a news channel which is open 24*7. Interview was scheduled in different slots due to higher numbers of candidates applying and mine has been scheduled at 6 pm. I will reach on time," I answered. "

"Ok, fine," he said.

****

After bouncers of questions, I left for my destination. It was all my heart's call and I was following it.

After 30 minutes of drive, I reached Kodak apartment, Noida Sector-85.

There were offices of several companies in that ten-storied building.

I took help from the signboard, which indicated that the Xpress News office was at the ground floor.

I reached at 5:30 pm.

I was standing in front of the office. I waited there for half an hour then got into the coffee house, which was close to the office.

I sat there in the direction of the office exit gate so that I could notice her if she passed from there.

I was lost and continuously looking outside the glass window of the coffee house towards the exit gate of the Xpress News office.

"Sir!, What would you like to have?" asked the waiter.

I ordered a Vanilla Cappuccino. It had been hours that I was sitting inside the coffee shop and had drunk lots of coffee.

I already spend all my money on coffee and had nothing to spend now.

At 9 pm, when finally it was time for the coffee shop to be shut, I moved out. I was quite disappointed.

I guess, I lost my senses that I was being crazy for something that did not belong to me.

Some people call it infatuation; some call it love at first sight. Whatever it was, I was just following my heart, which gave me happiness. I left the place after spoiling my mood and time.

However, this was not enough for the day. The real trouble started when my scooter stopped at Lajpat Nagar flyover as the fuel tank got empty. I had no money. Therefore, I had no choice, except pulling the scooter to my home. My home was 8 km away.

Chapter 7– Rainy Day

* * *

I could not sleep properly last night, but still managed to wake up early. After getting up, I switched on the TV immediately and tuned into Xpress News channel. I did not see her on the news channel as well, so I decided to go to her office again.

It was a rainy day. Dark, smoky clouds thundered at its best. It was 8 am, but was dark outside. Dense black clouds covered the city sky and it was raining heavily since night. The city was messed up with the heavy traffic jam. Schools were closed.

Despite the bad weather, my heart had an obsession to have a glimpse of her. So again, I could not resist my feelings and followed my heart. I prepared myself to sustain in the rainy weather. I wore a raincoat and again left for the Noida Sector 85, The Kodak apartment.

The city roads were converted into a small canal. There was a heavy traffic jam. I could not find any other two-wheeler expect mine.

Some said it right, "When we are in love, we do many nonsense things that we don't realize." I was doing the same. That is why it is called love is blind. Moreover, in my case, it was completely blind, I thought while I was stuck in the jam.

Traffic moved at the pace of a snail. I was all drenched and even the raincoat could not help me much. I managed to reach my destination after struggling for a few hours.

Today even the coffee house was also shut. I guess it must be because of the rainy weather.

I was standing under the open sky and getting

wet. The rain stopped. I waited for her outside the building, but could not see her coming out.

I could not resist myself and reached the office reception.

"Excuse me sir," the security Guard stopped me.

"Sir, to whom do you want to meet," he asked.

"Ananya Sen," I replied.

"Oh! Ananya Madam," he repeated her name.
"Yes" I nodded.

"Sir, she is on leave for last two or three days as she is unwell," he replied. "Can you please tell me when she will join?" I asked him curiously.

"Sir, I did not know, but she will join soon after getting well as she hardly takes leaves," said the guard.

I had no choice besides leaving.

As I was wet since a long time, my body was shivering with cold, but I somehow managed to reach home.

As I entered, my dad called me.

I have never been afraid of anything besides my dad.

"Adi..." he shouted.

"Yes dad," I replied.

"Where were you the whole day," he asked.

"Dad, I went for an interview," I was shivering while answering.

"The entire city was converted into a canal and roads were jam packed and you went for an interview? I cannot digest this. Either you think I am a fool to believe this or you are a fool. Tell the truth,"

he shouted.

He was angry. His raised eyebrows meant that he knew I was lying.

A father is always a father; he can read your lies and games.

I still tried to manage the situation.

"Dad, remember? Yesterday I went for an interview. So, today was the third round of the interview and I had to be there at any cost."

****

My clothes were wet and I was shivering. I had caught cold. I changed my clothes and dried my hair. I was not feeling well.

I was tired. I had wasted my whole day. I lay down on bed and random thoughts started flooding my brain. "Am I a fool that I am doing all the nonsense things for a girl whom I have never met? One, who even doesn't know about my existence, how would she react if I ever got a chance to meet her and when I tell her about all these foolish acts of mine?"

"I guess people in love are fools. I do not want to include myself in to that league. I went off to sleep."

Chapter 8–
Falling Apart

* * *

After a rainy day, it was a sunny morning. The sun's rays fell upon my bed and passed through the transparent shell of my attenuated body, warmed me, made me glow like a crystal. I felt sick and weak. I wanted to sleep more. I was lying on my bed. My mobile phone rang. I looked at the mobile screen.

Abhilasha had made a WhatsApp group, including Ajay, and Abhimanyu and I.

I smiled as it was a refreshing and exciting start of the day.

The name of the group was "Under Root 4A" which means four names starting with the letter "A".

Abhilasha: Hello everyone.
How are you guys?

Ajay: Hey Abhilasha
I am good. What about you and Abhimanyu? It's been so long that we all spoke to each other. Feeling good.

Abhimanyu: Hello Ajay
All good bro.
Where are you? What are you doing these days?

Ajay: Same place brother, where you left me.
But, I have joined my dad's transport business and am travelling all

across India.

Abhilasha- That's good Ajay.
But where is Aditya?
What is he doing?

Ajay: He must be sleeping in his bedroom where we saw him last time.

Abhimanyu -(laughed) Yeah sure.

Abhilasha- (laughed)
Good one Ajay

Now it's my turn to get into the conversation.

Me: Hi everyone. I am not sleeping.
Btw...
How are you all.
I really miss you all a lot.
I am so happy talking to you all after a long time.

Abhilasha: Same here Adi

Abhimanyu: No more worries! We are coming back to India for a week.

Me: Okie. Thank you guys.
You made my day with this news.
I am so excited to meet you all.

Ajay: But when?

Abhilasha: We are coming on Sunday guys.

Me: I cannot wait anymore.

We planned our meeting during the conversation and ended the chat.

I was happy and excited to meet my friends. However, right now, I did not want to wake up. I did not want to get out of the bed. I just wanted to go away or disappear.

Chapter 9 – Togetherness

❄ ❄ ❄

Two days passed and four more days were left. My wait for Sunday was not ending. At least I had a reason to smile.

It was difficult for me to pass my day, I kept myself busy by watching Xpress News channel just to see her. I had not come out of my room since Monday, and it was Friday today.

My parents were also worried after seeing me confined to my room and staying quiet.

In-between, my dad did inspection like before and asked me the reason for my disappointment.

I lied to him. I know lying to your parents is bad, but I had no choice.

I told him that continuous rejection in interviews frustrated me and put my morale down. I am preparing more and then I will go for the interviews.

****

Finally, the day had come when Abhilasha and Abhimanyu landed at the Airport. Abhilasha checked in on her Facebook profile.

As per our plans, we were going for a night out. Ajay picked up all of us and finally we met.

Moreover, we met in a style. We put our palm on each other's palm and started singing.

"Ye dosti hum nahi todenge, todenge dum magar, tera sath na chodenge."

We hugged each other for more than a minute. It was an emotional moment for all of us.

After all, we had reunited after a long time.

We had a lot of stuff to share with each other.

Ajay opened a champagne bottle.

Stars were twinkling brightly and it seemed that even the universe was celebrating with us.

We were on a traffic-free highway in a speeding car. Our music playlist was at its best.

Me: Thank you guys for coming and giving me a reason to cheer up after a long time.

Abhilasha: Thank you for what dumbo? I was also eager to meet you.

Abhimanyu: Yes guys.

Abhimanyu backed Abhilash's statement.

Abhimanyu:We missed our college days and the days we spent together.

Ajay said, "Tell us about your college life in the US and that too without us."

He turned his neck towards the back seat as we were sitting behind and he was on the diver seat.

Abhilasha asked him to focus on driving.

In addition, she started telling us about her college in the US and her amazing life in the States.

Abhimanyu also gave his input after Abhilasha completed. We talked about all that had happened with each one of us during the last six months.

We were now far from the city noise.

Abhilasha ended her conversation by saying, “Guys I have one more thing to tell you, but later, not now.”

“What’s that?” Ajay asked curiously.

Abhimanyu stared at Abhilasha and she immediately changed her statement.

I got the clue that she was hiding something.

Therefore, I forced her to tell us.

“It’s a secret that I will tell you when the perfect time arrives,” she said.

Ajay speeded up and increased the volume of the Punjabi songs.

He stopped the car somewhere near the bank of the Yamuna River.

The cold breeze relaxed me and made me forget all the troubles.

“This is the perfect place to stay,” I said.

Abhilasha was drunk enough to get out of control. Abhimanyu kept her tightly in his arms.

“Hey guys do you want to know the secret that I was talking about earlier,” she shouted.

Abhimanyu again stared at Abhilasha. It seemed like he wanted to hide something that Abhilasha wanted to tell us.

“Shut up,” Abhilasha shouted at Abhimnayu.

“They are my best friends and they must know all my secrets, “she explained.

“Ok fine, don’t be angry,” Abhimanyu replied politely.

"Me and Abhimanyu are no more good friends, "she said.

She was fumbling, as she was drunk.

"Me and Abhimanyu are in a relationship, "she said.

They then kissed each other.

I closed my eyes and Ajay was too bold to watch them intimate.

"Congratulations to both of you," Ajay interrupted them.

This was shocking for me as my bestie was in relationship with one of my friend.

"If I had been good at studies, she would be my girlfriend." I thought.

"For everything in life, you have to pay a cost." I thought.

The pain of being a failure and being good at nothing stabbed my soul, but I managed to control my emotions and congratulated them.

"I also want to tell you about my lady love," I said in full swing.

"Hey dude, you never told me about this," Ajay said surprisingly.

"We are in the same city. At least you should have arranged a meeting with Bhabhi Ji," he said angrily.

"I am also struggling to meet her," I told him with a low voice and my eyes were full of tears.

"Adi, are you kidding. How someone can be your love until you meet her," said Abhilasha.

"I am crazy for her. Whenever I see her, my heart beats faster. She is so pretty and adorable, "I said.

Ajay and Abhimanyu started laughing. They must be thinking that I was either drunk or I was telling a lie.

"Where did you meet her for the first time?" Ajay asked.

"I have never met her," I said.

They laughed at me again.

"Guys, I saw her on a News channel for the first time. I am a victim of love at first sight."

"I tried many times to meet her by visiting her office, but did not succeed. She does not know about me, but hopefully one day I will meet her and express my feelings, "I explained to them.

"And then..." There was silence for a few seconds.

Abhilasha started laughing all her heart out followed by Abhimanyu and Ajay.

They laughed together for a while.

This made me little uncomfortable.

"Are you mad, Adi," said Abhilasha. "You are wasting your time and emotions for a girl whom you have never met and who doesn't even know about you. Just focus on your life and career. Do not follow her," said Abhilasha.

"Moreover, she is not your lady love. It is just an infatuation which will end soon," said Abhilasha.

Now they all had a reason to tease me. They made fun of me. However, we enjoyed our togetherness.

We came back home early in the morning.

Chapter 10– A Long Chase

* * *

Time flies so quickly. It has been a week since Abhilasha and Abhimanyu went back to Boston to resume their studies.

Ajay got busy in his transport business. However, my life was still the same.

I was followed the same routine and continued watching the Xpress News channel for hours.

I had become a victim of depression.

I hesitated to get out of my bed or leave the house. I distant myself from people and do not meet them.

I felt worse during the morning and better at night.

I often cried and thought about suicide.

I was not good in studies, so I could not go for higher education. I don't have any family business.

I was going through the most difficult phase of my life and there was a new challenge.

Abhilasha told me that I was wasting my time on the newsreader and they all laughed at me.

I guess they were right. Had I been in their place, I would also have the same feedback.

****

It was early in the morning. I was watching my favorite News Channel. I saw her after a long time.

Her glimpse made me the world's happiest person at that moment. In that instant I forgot about all my pain, failures and even my purpose of life.

My only purpose was to meet her somehow.

While seeing her on the TV I realized that

she was not in the newsroom, but was reporting from somewhere in Delhi-NCR about the traffic problems during the rainy season.

I tried to recognize the place. She was at the bus stand near AIIMS, Delhi.

This was the best opportunity to meet her. I kick started my dad's scooter to reach there.

I reached Aurobindo Marg but got stuck in heavy traffic. My destination was not far but I had no choice but to wait. I then decided to leave my scooter and started running towards the bus stand near AIIMS. It was about a kilometer away.

After running for more than half of the distance, she was visible to my eyes.

But my bad luck followed me everywhere. She boarded her vanity van and left the place in front of me. I started running after the cab, following her and called her name 'Ananya' many times.

I obviously couldn't chase the cab, but she looked out of the window and there was a possibility that she might have heard her name.

I stood there and kept on looking at the car until it disappeared in to thin air.

I then wet back home.

Someone said it correctly, 'Love is like a disease which gradually stops all your senses from functioning properly.'

Chapter 11–
The preparation

❄ ❄ ❄

Today's night was not the same.

There was silence everywhere, but my head was full of noise.

Many doubts and questions were stomping my head.

"Questions like failure in studies, career, being below average in everything, not being a good son, about my future, and what will I do in life," all these questions had occupied my mind.

I wanted answers to all my questions. I wanted to set a goal and move on in my life. I wanted to build a career like all my friends. I wanted to be the reason behind my father's smile. And I also wanted my love to be mine.

I was sitting in a corner of my room and continuously looked at the clock.

In addition, I decided to work hard to get a good job and then only I would approach the girl who stole my heart.

****

Next Morning

"Good morning papa," I greeted him.

"Good morning Adi," he replied.

However, he was shocked but his face expressed it all.

Obviously, he was surprised. This morning is different from all other mornings in the past. I woke up early today. That is what surprised him.

As per my planning, I updated my resume on the job portal and called some hiring consultants to schedule my interviews.

This was the new life, which I had planned for myself, but more struggles were waiting to for me.

Even in times of such anxiousness, something gave me the energy and positivity to fight and win.

I started giving interviews at every alternate day. Every failure in the interview gave me a reason to improve my skills.

I already had given dozens of interviews, but did not get any job. This was something, which made me feel sad, but I always tried to motivate myself and prepare for my next interview with the same enthusiasm.

Motivational posters covered the walls in my room.

My posters read:

'Failure will never overtake me if my determination to succeed is strong enough.'

'Expect problems and eat them for breakfast.'

'In order to succeed, we must first believe that we can.'

'Success is no accident. It is hard work, perseverance, learning, studying, sacrifice and most of all, love of what you are doing or learning to do.'

"Set your sights high, the higher, and the better. Expect the most wonderful things to happen, not in the future, but right now. Realize that nothing is too good. Allow absolutely nothing to hamper you or hold you up in any way.'

My most favorite quotation of all was 'Winners

Never Quit & Quitters Never Win.'

After struggling for a month, my hard work and determination paid off.

I got a job in a reputed bank as a sales executive. I was so happy. My job role was to sell loans. It was not a typical 9 to 5 job, but a sales job in this field with monthly targets to achieve. At last, a positive move knocked my life. I became successful in my own way.

Chapter 12–
Office Hours

* * *

After college, it was a new phase of my life. My job included field visits. I had to go out in the sun and work in areas where pollution was high. It was really difficult and challenging for a person like me to handle it, but I had no choice but to accept it. Despite all difficulties, the exciting part of my job was my office location. It was in the same building where Ananya's office was located i.e. Kodak apartment, Sector-85, Noida. This was one of the reasons that I had joined the organization.

I left for office every day with a hope to meet her.

"Ananya Sen" the lovely lady, controlled me and motivated me to be a successful person. She had no clue about the effect she had on me.

I cannot deny the fact that my desire to get her and my love for her helped me get out of my comfort zone to do something meaningful in my life.

I reached office on time and took briefings about the products. I attended all the meetings and left for the field visits for the assigned clients.

However, before leaving for client meetings, I made it a point to have coffee at my favourite place.

I followed the same routine every day in a hope that one day she might come to the coffee house and I could share my feelings to her.

****

The days passed gradually and I spent them the same way. Every day I stopped at the coffee house for hours just in a hope to meet her one day.

Love is crazy. You can't even think rationally that what is good or bad for you. You just follow your heart irrespective of everything. This is what was happening with my life.

Days turned into weeks and weeks became months, but I could not see her. I spent half of my first salary on coffee.

That was the only hope to see her. With each passing day, my determination grew stronger. Meeting her now became one of my dreams.

****

On the other hand, my professional life was also not going good. I had completed more than one month with the bank, but could not find a single client. I always felt insulted at the daily meetings whenever my boss asked me questions about my daily achievements.

Like every morning, I left for office and after the meeting; I came and sat at the coffee shop before going out for client meeting. I choked with the first sip of coffee, not because the coffee was hot but due to the pain that my longing for Ananya brought about.

She entered the coffee shop with few of her friends and sat on the table adjacent to me. She looked phenomenal in a red suit. I could not take my eyes off her. She was a complete goddess. She was in front of me. It was just like a dream come true. I was looking at her from the corner of my eyes.

I always thought that the day I meet her, I would express my feelings to her, But her presence froze my lips and my heartbeat went erratic.

I finished the coffee and walked towards the

counter to order another. I passed by her table. They were gossiping and laughing. Her smile was contagious.

I returned to my table and tried to gather courage to start a conversation with her.

They finished their coffee and were about to leave. That was exactly the kind of opportunity I was looking for, since such a long time. I could not just let it go waste.

Therefore, I also stood up and called out her name.

She looked back.

"Yes" she said.

I got closer to her and introduced myself.

"Hi! My name is Aditya. I am a sales officer working with Yes Bank."

She was no more interested in talking to me as she gave me a weird look.

"How may I help you?" she asked.

"Actually, our bank is giving a few offers on its anniversary on loans. If you or any of your friends need loan, let me know."

"Sorry, I didn't need anything," she replied.

"Ok! No problem," I said.

You can take my card. Whenever you need any of our bank services, you can contact me.

She took my visiting card, said ok, and walked outside.

She unexpectedly returned and asked, "By the way Mr. Aditya, how do you know my name?" She raised a valid question.

"From the TV channel you work for," I

answered.

"I am big fan of your news reading," I said.

She smiled and left.

Chapter 13–
Under performance

* * *

It was more than a month since I had joined the office. Today was the performance review day for the last month. I was sure that I would be the worst performer. The mere thought of it made my heart sink.

I did not have any clue about, how my boss would react. Whatever it would be, I have to face the truth at last.

As usual, I reached office on time. All my colleagues were already present and waiting for my boss, Aniket. So finally, the wait was over and Aniket came in the meeting room, took the podium and greeted all of us.

Hi, team. As you know, today we have a monthly performance review.

I guess you all must be excited?" he asked.

Only a few raised their voice in a "YES" and the rest kept mum.

"I know you all are champions, except a few. This few must be for me, I thought.

He opened his laptop and started showing performance graph for each one of us.

The name of the top three performers was in green, the names of mediocre performers were in yellow and the poor performers highlighted in red. However, my name was in blue color. It was only my name, which was in blue.

While looking at my name in the chart, I thought that today was the day, when I would be asked to leave for being the non-performer for the month.

Aniket started calling the names from the top of the list.

Top performers were recognized. I was feeling uncomfortable, as my turn was getting closer.

All the officers present in the meeting room were notified of their performance review and thus left. I wondered that why my name was not being called out. I was afraid of losing my job.

Then Aniket walked up to me and offered me to have coffee with him. We went to the coffee house.

"Aditya, do you have any family problem or any other personal reason which is not letting you focus on your job?" he asked.

"No problem sir. Everything is fine."

"Are you not serious or not liking your job," he fired one more question.

There was silence for the next minute.

I did not know what to answer. I kept calm, took a sip of coffee and then replied to him, "Sir I am new in marketing field, so it is difficult to sell products, but please believe in my abilities, I will prove my worth to the company."

I put in all my efforts to convince him that I will give better performance further.

"I believe in you that's why I hired you," he said.

"Sir, I will give my best from now onwards." I promised.

"That's the spirit boy. Well, I am looking forward to your performance improvement. Good luck," he wished me.

We ended the conversation on a happy note and then left the place.

Chapter 14–
Unofficial Chat

* * *

At Home
2 am
Sunday

I lay down on my bed, tried hard to sleep, but my mind did not let me rest.

There is this thing with me that as soon as I hit my bed, I am unable to sleep. I start thinking about where my life decisions.

I was searching something on Google. I typed and then deleted what I wrote. I did it many times.

I was looking for answers to questions like-

What should be the marketing strategy?

How to convince the customers?

And so on.

In-between, I also tried finding answers to important questions like how to impress a girl.

Passing through this turmoil in the middle of the night, my mobile phone beeped with a Whatsapp alert.

I had received a message from an unknown number.

It looked like one of my friend's number.

To confirm, I checked the profile picture and I was surprised to see it. The message was from my dream girl.

Yes, it was from Ananya.

Ananya: Hi

Me: Hi Ananya. How are you?

Ananya: I am fine. What about you?
Sorry for disturbing you at this time.
I saw you online, so I pinged you.

Me: That is ok. No Problem.

Ananya: I need your help as you work in a bank.
Right?

Me: Yes, I am! How can I help you?

Ananya: I am from Kolkata and I am living as a paying guest here. My parents wanted to move to Delhi with me, as I am their only child. Therefore, I want to buy a new flat in Delhi-NCR and for that, I need home loan. Can you help me with this?

Me: Of course, I will definitely help you.
Do not worry.

Ananya: Can we meet tomorrow, if you have time?
I had waited for this for so long now that I could not believe what she had said.

Me: Sure

Ananya: So, let's meet at 1 pm tomorrow at the coffee house.

Me: Done.

Ananya: Thank you very much.

Me: You are welcome.

Ananya: Ok then. See you tomorrow. Good Night

Me: Good Night

This situation reminded me of SRK's film dialogue from OM SHANTI OM.

"When you want something, the universe conspires to help you achieve it."

During the entire conversation, I wanted to tell her about my feelings for her.

However, you need to be someone's friend first, only then you can be a lover.

In addition, I have to follow that and until then I have to wait for the perfect time.

I then had a sound sleep.

Chapter 15–
First Official Meeting

* * *

Next Morning, I woke up early.

My first thought of the day was meeting Ananya.

I was dressed in a black suit with white shirt and a red tie and also put on some fragrance to smell nice.

Here I was, ready to make my first impression.

Kodak Apartment, Noida

I reached office on time. As always, I took the briefings first and met my boss, Aniket.

I had a long discussion with him about the marketing strategies.

He shared some of his experiences when he was new in the banking sector.

I wanted to make good use of his experience in client handling techniques, as I did not want to lose Ananya as my client. That was the only way I could meet her often and it was my only hope of being friends with her.

Coffee House

I was sitting at the corner table of the cafe. It was 12:45 p.m. I was excited to meet her. Every passing minute gave me eternal happiness.

My eyes were stuck on the entry gate of the cafe. Finally, my wait was over. She entered the coffee house sharp at 1p.m. As always, she looked beautiful in her traditional attire.

She was beautiful, and had sparkling eyes. Her simplicity attracted me the most.

I waved my hand to her. She noticed me and came to share the table with me.

The girl, for whom I was crazy, was finally

sitting with me. I was nervous and it was embarrassing as there were no words that came out of my mouth.

I still motivated myself.

"Hi Aditya," she said and extended her hand for a handshake.

"Hi Ma'am," I replied.

"My Name is Ananya, so please call me by my name," she said with a smile.

"Ok ma'am. Sorry Ananya," I replied.

"How may I help you in purchasing a new flat?" I asked.

"I want to buy a flat within a budget of 35 lakh rupees. I need home loan for the same. As I am new in Delhi, and I don't have much idea about all this, so I need your help," she said.

"It is my core job and of course I will help you in finding a suitable flat as well as will assist you with the home loan."

I showed her a catalog of few societies, which were ready to move in apartments. She showed interest in a few and wanted to visit the location.

I explained to her the process of the loan and the documents required for it.

She ordered a cold coffee and I ordered the same. Although, I do not like cold coffee, but just to pretend that we had common likings, I ordered one too.

We continued our conversation for the next couple of hours.

She was the most talkative girl I had ever met.

I have heard that Bengali girls are extremely

friendly. They are bold and courageous, and they do not wait for you to make a move. In addition, she was proving it right.

In addition, her eyes were beautiful and expressive. Those were the eyes; you could just stare all day long and get lost in a magical world.

I never wanted to end our conversation, but I had to as she had to continue with her day's tasks.

At the end of the meeting, we decided to visit a few flats, but were still to plan the day for it.

Chapter 16–
A Funny Shit

❄ ❄ ❄

It was a Sunday. I was in the washroom and my phone vibrated and fell in the pot. I could not take it out, but I could only see Ananya's name flashing on the wet screen.

I did not know why Ananya had called me.

She might want to meet me or just wanted to talk to me.

Without a second thought, I immediately planned to meet her at her office.

****

I reached Xpress news office. The guard did not allow me to enter the office without permission. I told him that I wanted to meet Ananya. However, he enquired several questions. At last, he got convinced. After a few minutes, he got back to me and allowed me to wait in the reception area.

"Ananya madam is busy and will be free only after half an hour," he told me.

I sat on the sofa in the reception while waiting for her.

My eyes were stuck on the wall clock and every minute felt like an hour.

Soon my wait was over. I heard Ananya's voice, calling my name.

She wore a red and white Patiala suit. She looked fabulous in her attire.

"Sorry Aditya that you had to wait for me," she apologized.

"Hey, no problem," I replied while smiling.

"I am free now for the whole day, so if you have time can we go and look for apartments that you had shown me. I called you, but you didn't take my call," she said.

Then I told her the story of my phone falling into the pot.

She burst into innocent crackling laughter.

After sometime, we then left her office.

We reached my favorite coffec house. Ordered our coffee and planned for the day.

We decided to go to 'Greater Noida West' as I had prepared a list of ready-to-move in apartments in that location.

Chapter 17–
A Long Drive

❄ ❄ ❄

We were on our way to Greater Noida. Ananya was driving her Santro car. It was sunny, but clouds hovered upon the sky soon and it started raining.

The weather was pleasant and romantic. To my surprise, even the radio played a romantic number.

I broke the silence.

"What a timing, rain and romantic song on a long drive," she said.

"Is it?" I asked.

"Yeah! It is," she shook her head.

"Do you have a boyfriend?" I asked just to continue the conversation.

She frowned looking at me and replied, "No"

"Really," I asked her to confirm. A wave of happiness ran in my veins.

"Of course," she replied immediately.

It was adorable and I loved the way she replied.

"I don't believe that a beautiful girl like you is still single.

Is it by choice or by chance," I asked her.

She laughed and replied, "I didn't find anyone perfect, who could steal my heart."

"That means I still have a chance on you," I tried to flirt.

She laughed and replied, "My heart is protected under deep layers."

"I bet you, I have the keys that can open hearts and then I can steal it," I said while grinning.

****

We reached the Apex apartments in Greater Noida.

Apartments are located in the prime sectors of Noida and within the reach of the metro station. We were on the 18th floor of the apartment and could see the vast greenery spread across.

We visited a few more apartments nearby.

After searching for a flat the whole day, we were tired and headed back to our homes.

Chapter 18– Friendship Blossoms

❄ ❄ ❄

For the next couple of weeks, whenever Ananya and I had time, we visited different localities, met the builders to find a suitable flat for her. We started meeting frequently. Due to these meetings, we also started talking over the phone. We kept in touch throughout the day.

No matter what was the purpose of our first meeting, but we were best friends now.

I cannot imagine a day without talking to her.

We started hanging out at different places in the city. We both loved to watch animation movies and never missed any new release.

With each passing day, my love and emotions for Ananya were only getting stronger and deeper. However, I didn't have the courage to confess my love for her. I never wanted to be friend zoned, but I was scared to lose her friendship.

Each day I asked the same question to myself.

It is difficult for a person to act as a friend when he actually loves a girl.

****

Within a month, I finally succeeded helping her in purchasing a flat of her choice.

Ananya was happy with her new home where she was planning to move in with her parents.

"Thank you Aditya," she said over the call.

"Hey, no need to be thankful. It's my duty as a friend," I said.

"Aditya, I am free from office work now and if you have time, can we meet today," she asked politely.

I was out for an important client meeting, but who cares, because if a beautiful girl offers you such a proposal, you always say yes.

Without even giving it a second thought, I said, "Yes".

We decided to meet at 5, in the evening at the coffee house just outside her office.

I reached before time and took a seat in the corner.

When she came, I couldn't help but be lost in her beauty. She always looked pretty, but this time she wore a western dress. Blue jeans and a pink top, I had never seen her like that. She had the magic to steal anybody's heart in her new look.

While I was lost in her beauty, she stood near me and pinched my cheeks with her sharp nails.

"Ouch," I screamed in pain.

She laughed and I just smiled sheepishly.

"Hello Mr. Banker, are you lost in someone's thoughts or busy staring at pretty girls in the café," she said.

I wanted to hug her and tell her about my feelings. I wanted to tell her the truth, but I did not have the guts to risk my friendship with her.

"I was thinking about you," I murmured.

You know, girls can actually sense about what is going on in a boy's mind.

We started sharing about our families, our friends, our dreams and a lot of other personal information. We also began to feel caring for each other.

We ordered our favorite coffee and started with our gossips. She was unstoppable once she started talking. I loved listening to her chitter-chatter.

I never found her boring.

She was naughty at times and sometimes she would act like a kid and get angry. She had always been a reason for my happiness.

"Can we go for a movie tonight," she asked.

I agreed immediately and booked two tickets for 10 to1 am show.

Only three hours were left for the movie to start. Going back home and then coming back again for the movie did not seem to be a good idea. Therefore, we decided to stroll on the road.

After a few meters of walk, we found some food stalls. She grabbed my hand and dragged me to a pani-puri stall.

Ananya ordered two plates of pani-puri, but I denied, so she cancelled one plate, but forced me to taste from her's.

She again requested to which I could not deny. She started feeding me from her own hands. Once I started eating from her hands, I forgot the count of the number of pani-puris I ate.

Suddenly, she put small pieces of green chilies in pani-puri and the moment I ate, my mouth went numb. My nose was red and eyes were filled with water.

"You fatso, how many will you eat?" she shouted amusingly.

"First you denied eating and now you have

eaten more than me," she taunted.

"If I have a chance to eat from your hands, I would eat until you don't stop feeding me," I replied.

"Ok Mr. Banker," she said while tapping my head and smiled looking into my eyes.

****

We didn't realize that we had reached some unfamiliar market area, far from where we started.

We reached a local market and Ananya entered a bag shop.

"Bhaiya, how much is this red bag for?" she asked the storekeeper.

"Rs 500 Madam," replied the shopkeeper.

"No bhaiya it is costly." she stared bargaining.

All of a sudden, she came to me and said something in my ears, which was actually too faint to be audible to the human ear.

She held my hand and said to the shopkeeper, "Bhaiya, my husband thinks that it is expensive. His friend got the same bag for 200 rupees for his wife."

I was stunned after listening to what she had just said to the shopkeeper.

Then, I understood the reason that she actually did not say anything into my ears. It was just to fool the shopkeeper.

A man can never understand a woman. They all are a unique mystery in their own. I instead enjoyed the moment.

"Babuji, Madam likes the bag, please don't think about the money, buy it," the shopkeeper said to me.

Before I could reply, Ananya asked him, "Bhaiya, if you want to sell it for 200, tell us."

Finally, Ananya bought it for 250.

A boy can never do such bargaining and buy a product at half the price.

She bought a Laughing Buddha and gifted to me.

"It will fulfill all your wishes," she said.

She may never know that out of all my wishes, winning her love was one of the most precious one.

Chapter 19–
Night out

* * *

It was around 10 pm. We reached the cinema hall.

The hall was empty, with only a few couples seated in the corner seats.

We took our seat, which was at the center.

I tried focusing on the movie screen, but a few couples around us distracted me.

Ananya tapped my head and gestured me to look at the screen.

I was a little uncomfortable where we sat, so I requested Ananya to change our seats, as plenty of them were vacant.

While watching the movie, I kept looking at Ananya's face. She caught me once, smiled, and asked me to look towards the screen and not her face.

I again tried to focus on the movie.

Suddenly, I realized that she had put her hand on mine. I felt the warmth of her touch. I opened my eyes and looked towards her face. She was engrossed in watching the movie. I didn't understand, whether it was intentional or an unintentional move from her. I didn't react but enjoyed the beauty of the moment.

The movie got finished at 1:30 am and we got out of the theatre.

****

It was 1:30 am and we were walking alongside the road. The weather was pleasant. We were walking slowly and quietly.

"Aren't you scared of staying out of your home this late at night?" I asked her.

"I feel safe as long as you are with me," she replied.

I could see her sparking eyes.

Her eyes revealed all the things that her lips could not.

"So give me a lifetime responsibility of protecting you," I said.

"Really?" She chuckled.

"Stealing my heart is not that easy, let us keep our friendship busy," she replied in a rhyme.

"I will steal your heart in a blink of an eye, don't blame me girl, when you get a surprise," I replied in a similar way.

We were walking on the roadside and suddenly a few bikers passed us. Ananya got scared and panicked, fell over me, and hugged me tightly.

"Are you ok," I asked her.

She looked adorable. I wanted to kiss her forehead and let her know that I would protect her for the rest of my life. However, I knew my limits.

****

We returned to our respective homes.

It was five in the morning and I could not sleep. I was thinking about Ananya and the time spent with her.

I could still feel her touch.

I kept looking at the Laughing Buddha she gifted me.

She was the kind of beauty that gently fell on the lips like snowflakes, silent, subtle, fragile to touch, but beautiful nonetheless.

My phone vibrated and I received a text message from her, which read- 'I am happy to have a gem of a person like you in my life... Thank You.'

Chapter 20–
Shifting Flat

❄ ❄ ❄

Soon after Ananya got the keys of her new flat, she planned to move in with her old parents who were staying in Kolkata.

She called me to inform that her parents were coming to Delhi next Sunday and requested me to join her to receive them at the airport.

However, she wanted to shift to her new flat before they came. We were thus busy shifting for the next few days. She purchased lots of stuff for her new house.

She decorated the house like a professional interior designer. She placed each item according to Vaastu. She had placed the sofa and cabinets in the south-west direction and she placed decorative pieces and flower decorations in the northeast direction. She had also purchased an aquarium, which she kept opposite the entrance of the hall.

****

It was Sunday morning and we reached the airport to receive her parents.

"Hey Adi, look, my father is waving his hand and that is my mother standing is next to him," she said.

I started waving towards the crowd, but got confused, as I couldn't make out who her parents were out of all the people there. Ananya hugged her parents and hinted me to greet them.

I touched their feet and they gave me blessings.

"Papa, he is Aditya, my best companion in Delhi," she told her father.

"I knew beta, you always talk about him. We

already guessed it when we saw you with him," her father replied.

Ananya smiled looking into my eyes.

I was sure that she also had the same feelings as I have for her.

"I love her and she loves me too."

****

I messaged my friend Abhilasha on Whatsapp to solve the problem of my confused heart.

"Hi Abhilasha," I messaged her.

"Hi boy, how are you Dog? You forgot us since you find your blind love," she teased me.

"So tell me, how is all with life? At least reply now," she further added.

"First you abuse me as much as you like, I will then reply."

"I am done with them all," she laughed.

I also laughed.

"Now tell me the progress of your love life and professional life," she asked.

"All good, but I need your help."

"No worries. Tell me," Abhilasha replied.

"I don't know what to do. I love Ananya, but do not have courage to tell her about my feelings. I observe her actions and expressions and I am sure that she loves me too and has feelings for me."

I told Abhilasha everything.

"I have an Idea to solve your problem."

"What?"

"Take her love test."

"What love test?"

She detailed me about everything.

"It's a brilliant Idea. Thank you, you have solved half my problem," I told her.

I decided to take Ananya's love test the very next day.

Chapter 21–
Love Test

* * *

I took leave from office and planned to stay at home. I did not send Ananya a good morning message that I used to send her every morning. I put my cell on flight mode so that no one could contact me.

The day passed. I missed Ananya and wanted to hear her voice but I controlled myself, as I wanted to know about her feelings.

To keep myself busy I started watching Xpress news to get a glimpse of her lovely face.

Time passed quickly. It was 8 p.m. I finally decided to switch from my flight mode to network mode. My phone started buzzing continuously. There were 39 missed call alerts and around 20 messages. All the alerts were from Ananya.

1st Message: 8 a.m.
Good morning Adi

2nd Message: 8:15 a.m.
Good Morning Mr. Banker

3rd Message: 9:00 a.m.
Still Sleeping?

4th Message: 9:20 a.m.
Hello Mr., at least reply me once.

5th Message: 10:40 a.m.
I will be busy in office until 3p.m. So, I will not be able to pick your call. Please message me once you read my messages.
If you are free, then please meet me

at the coffee house after three, I will
be there.
See you, Miss you.

6th Message: 3:15 p.m.
Hey. How was your day?
Is everything ok?

7th Message: 5 p.m.

Where were you the whole day?
I called u several times, but your phone was out of reach.
I called at your office number, but they told me that you were on leave today.
Adi please call me asap. I am worried now.
Miss u…

The list of messages was long. I was busy reading each one of them. All of a sudden, my phone started ringing and it was none other than Ananya's call.

I picked up the phone and before I could speak, she started shouting at me.

I kept mum and listened to her intently.

I could feel the anger in her voice, but at the same time, it carried so much love and care.

She kept asking me questions for another 10 minutes. However, I replied in single words like sorry, *Hmm.*

Slowly, her anger turned into a polite conversation. I did not say much, but let her calm down.

Moreover, I successfully took her love test, which she passed.

Now, I was sure that she too missed me when I was not around.

****

"I want to meet you right now. I am still in my office. Please come here as soon as possible," she demanded.

I reached her office. She came out of the office building. She smiled by looking at me and I smiled back at her. She hugged me and murmured in my ears, "Never, do this to me ever again."

"Never," I promised.

She kissed on my cheeks and left a mark of her lipstick.

I got nervous because of such a gesture at a public place. However, I was very happy within.

Later, she wiped the lipstick mark with a tissue.

Her eyes were brimming with tears, but she controlled her emotions. I knew that the tears in her eyes were for me.

However, I never wanted to be a reason for her sadness.

I invited her for dinner at my home, to which she agreed.

I called my mom asked her to cook delicious food as I had invited a friend.

I didn't tell her that my friend was a girl or her would be daughter-in-law.

She sat on my scooter's back seat and we headed home. I rang the doorbell.

"Please wait, coming," shouted my mom.

As she opened the door, she was surprised to see an unfamiliar girl with me.

She only knew about Abhilasha as my only friend.

"Is she your friend? I thought you were inviting your college best friends," mom said.

"Yes, mom she is my best friend. Her name is Ananya Sen," I introduced her to my mother.

"*Namaste* Aunty *ji*," Ananya greeted my mom.

"Namaste *beta*," she replied.

"She is just your friend or a girlfriend," my mom enquired.

Ananya laughed and replied, "Aunty we are just best friends. I am not his girlfriend."

"But *beta* you are a girl and his friend. So, indirectly you are his girlfriend," And they both laughed.

"I know he cannot propose to a girl. He is only busy doing nonsense things. *He has never done anything sensible in his life other than making you a friend*," my mother taunted me and they both laughed hysterically.

While my mother was busy preparing dinner, I showed her some of my childhood photographs and shared some of my childhood memories with Ananya. We both shared many funny childhood stories with each other.

****

We all gathered at the dining table around 9 p.m.

I told Ananya that we had a fixed time for dinner, as my dad was disciplined and particular about meal hours.

I introduced her to my dad. He was happy to meet her and started conversing with her as she was a journalist too. He asked random questions to her and she answered all of them smartly.

My mom and dad were impressed after meeting her. She had a jolly nature and thus my dear Ananya did not take much time to get friendly with my parents. Dad also asked her about how we became friends. She told him about how we met for the first time and how I helped her in getting a new flat.

Later, I dropped Ananya at her home.

Chapter 22–
Birthday Bash

* * *

April 29, 2015
Sharp at 12 midnight

My phone started ringing continuously. My friends, cousins and relatives started calling me. I was waiting to hear only one voice.

Happy Birthday To You….
Happy Birthday To You….
Happy Birthday To dear Adi

My best friends Abhilasha, Abhimanyu and Ajay wished me first. They all were together on a conference call.

While I was talking to them, there was a call waiting from Ananya. I told them to hang up, so that I could receive her call.

They all started teasing me using her name.

"*Oho! Bhabhi Ji* calling," said Abhilasha.

"Now, why would you be interested in us," teased Ajay.

"Say hello to *Bhabhi Ji* on our behalf," they all shouted together.

Friends are really your world and without them, you cannot create memories. They are the ones, who understand the depth of your love for someone and still act silly.

Ananya was calling continuously. I picked her call.

Happy Birthday To You
Happy Birthday To my Dear Adi….

Her sweet voice echoed in my ears.

"Why were you are not picking up my call. I

wanted to wish you before anyone else. But you didn't let me," she said nonchalantly.

"Oh Baby, Don't mind," I replied.

"First my cousins and then my friends called me. As we spoke after a very long time, so I could not cancel their call," I explained.

"What is the plan for today?" She asked.

"I don't have any such plan, but if you take a leave from office, we will go to Agra," I replied.

"Yeah, sure, "she said excitedly.

"What do you want for your birthday?" she asked.

"A kiss," I replied.

"You dirty mind," she squealed.

"Yes, a kiss would be the perfect gift," I repeated.\

"Are you sure Mr. Banker?" she confirmed.

"Of course darling," I replied.

"You will have to pay the interest too," she said.

"No worries, anything for you."

We then discussed about our plan for Agra trip.

****

April 29, 2016

8 a.m.

I was sleeping and my phone rang.

It rang nonstop but I was in a deep sleep.

After sometime, someone had knocked the door of my room. I got up and opened the door, while rubbing my eyes.

Ananya was standing outside my room with a birthday cake in her hands. I smiled and wanted to hug her tightly, but I then realized that I was only wearing underwear, so I quickly moved back to my bed to cover myself.

She laughed at my pitiable situation.

"Didn't you sleep last night," I asked her.

"No, I didn't. If I had slept, I wouldn't have been able to wake up this early to give you a surprise," she said.

I asked her to wait for 15 minutes in the drawing room, so that I could freshen up. We then cut the cake and left for Agra in Ananya's car as per our plan.

Chapter 23– Endless reasons to love

❄ ❄ ❄

I had never been to Agra. However, I got a number of chances during my school and college days, but I did not go. After three hours of drive, we reached Agra.

We were tired, so we decided to rest in a hotel room and then go for an excursion. Later, we visited the Taj Mahal.

Our guide explained us the history of Taj Mahal.

It was our first trip together so I tried to make it memorable. We later visited many other palaces nearby. After dinner, we spent the night together at our hotel room.

We enjoyed our outing. She got closer to me and kissed my cheeks. She then hugged me gently.

We kissed each other again and made love.

"Please never leave me," she whispered while looking into my eyes.

"Never till my last breath," I said and kissed her forehead.

It was the best gift I had ever received on my birthday.

****

The next morning, I woke up early before the first rays of the sun could shine through the window. I saw Ananya sleeping beside me. She looked beautiful. I kissed her forehead, placed a letter and a bunch of roses on the table, and left the room.

My Love Ananya,

Falling in love is a leap of faith. I am glad that we both jumped for each other. I used to count the number of hours until I see you again.

Sleeping alone now sucks…

We always lose track of time when we are together. You are the first person with whom I want to share my life's highs and lows.

You find my weird habits adorable. I can be myself when I am with you. We both know that together we can work out anything.

You are the light of my life…

You are my inspiration…

We are a perfect match…

You understand me…

You are simply irresistible….

My love for you will only grow more with each passing day. I have endless reasons to love you, I cannot tell you all, but my love for you is pure, is sweeter than the God's food, Honey, and is deeper than the oceans.

I love you unconditionally.
Yours Only,
Aditya

****

I came outside the hotel room and started playing cricket with children in a nearby park. However, my heart was focused on the reaction she would have after reading my letter. I was excited, I was curious and I was a bit nervous as well. My heart was beating fast. It was just like, when I saw her first. I then heard her voice.

"Adi," she called me. I turned back and she was

just in front of me. She hugged me tight instantly that I did not get time for any reaction.

Kids around us started whistling.

"I love you too," she whispered in my ears.

Later, we started our journey back to Delhi.

Chapter 24–
Her Inspiration

❄ ❄ ❄

After 2 years

Ananya entered into my life when I had lost all hopes. She brightened up my life. She inspired me to become a better person. She always had a positive approach towards life. She taught me to smile, enjoy life, and hope for good in everyone, to love and to let love in. In fact, she inspired me to reach for my goals and never settle for less. Seeing her, gave me a reason to live with joy.

Life had changed a lot during the last few years. I was now a successful banker. She was a strong woman who helped me during my struggles and despite that; she did not leave me alone.

All these thoughts had kept me engrossed and I did not realize that Ananya had come to the coffee shop. She kissed my cheeks.

Now even I was comfortable with her sweet display of love in public. In fact, I loved it. She looked adorable while doing such crazy things. She looked into my eyes and smiled. All I could see in her eyes was my world.

"Hey, you told me that you have something urgent to discuss," I asked her.

"I have to discuss with you about our relationship," she said.

"It's good going baby. I love you more with each passing day," I said happily.

"I mean to take our relationship to the next level," she gave me a serious look.

"You mean, marriage," I asked.

"Yes, marriage," she replied without taking a pause.

"Let's go," I told her, while holding her hand.

"But, where?" she asked.

"To get married," I answered.

"Are you crazy Adi? I am talking about something serious and you are making fun of it," she said angrily.

"No, baby, I am serious too."

"No, you are not," she again popped up.

"I am."

"No, you are not."

"I am serious darling," I ensured her.

"No, you are not," she said.

We argued for the next couple of minutes. At last, she fell silent.

"Baby you are not looking good. Please smile," I broke the silence.

"Till the time you won't be serious, I will not talk to you," she said.

"Ok, I always thought it to be better once we get settled in our careers before getting married," I said.

"You are right Adi, I agree with you. I am not in a hurry, but my parents are. They want me to get married soon, so they have started looking for a match for me," she replied.

We had a long discussion on it and decided to tell our parents about our relationship.

Chapter 25–
Plan Execution

* * *

Scene-1

At my house on dining table

I was a little hesitant on how to start the conversation but I had to.

"Mom don't you think that you need a support in your daily work at home? I mean you need a daughter-in-law," I asked.

"Of course, beta. Your dad and I discuss daily about the same. We have even started looking for a suitable bride for you," she replied.

"But, you didn't ask me," I said.

"We didn't feel the need for it. When we find a perfect girl for you we will let you know."

"But won't it be better if you ask me, because may be I have already chosen someone."

"Do you have someone in your life?"

I hastily said, "Yes".

"Who?"

"Ananya, you know her."

"You mean that journalist girl?"

"Hmmm..." I nodded.

"It would be our pleasure if she becomes the bride of my son and we would love to her as our daughter-in-law."

My parents were happy upon hearing this.

"I hope you both have no problem with her," I asked for confirmation.

"Definitely, we don't have any problem, but what about her parents," dad asked.

"She will talk to them regarding the same and I

will let you know."

Scene-2

At Ananya's house on dining table

"Mom, have you found any match for me till now," Ananya asked.

"We have shortlisted a few profiles for you. Don't worry, we will choose wisely for you my darling," her mom replied.

After a few minutes of silence, Ananya asked again.

"Do you remember my best friend, Aditya?" she asked.

"Oh yes, he is a nice boy," her mother said and further asked, "What happened to him?"

"He is fine mom. He is now working as a branch manager in a bank."

"His parents are looking for a perfect match for him," she tried to give some hint to her mother.

"Good! Did he find anyone," her mom asked.

"Yes," Ananya replied.

"She must be a lucky girl. He is a decent boy."

With some hesitation, Ananya told her parents.

I actually love him and he loves me too. We have decided to live our life together. I cannot imagine my life without him. So, we have decided to marry," she finally told them.

His father broke his silence and said, "No Ananya! How can you marry a non-Bengali boy? This is not in our culture. This is against the tradition of our society."

He gave her a long lecture on tradition of their accentors, culture and social boundaries.

All of a sudden, the dinner table turned into a lecture hall, where Ananya's father was delivering a speech on tradition and family ethics.

Ananya did not argue with her father, but left the dining room and came back to her bedroom.

Tears rolled down her cheeks.

****

My phone rang. Ananya was calling.

"Hello Adi," her voice was dull.

"Hey baby, what happened?"

"Adi, I can't marry someone else. I love you so much," she cried.

"Yes baby, we would definitely get married," I consoled her.

"But, Adi....Adi...," she cried incessantly.

"Ananya please don't cry. We will be together forever," I tried to console her.

My efforts helped to finally calm her down.

She told me about her discussion with her parents.

"Everything will be fine. My parents have no problem and I am sure your parents will also accept us."

She was carefully listening to me as long as I was speaking and finally I made her smile.

****

In the next couple of weeks, we arranged a

meeting for our parents. Initially Ananya's parents had objection to our marriage, considering their family culture and tradition. However, we made efforts to have their permission.

Sometimes it seemed as if it would never happen as Ananya's father was a Bengali Brahmin and he was rigid about his ethics.

Ananya and I wanted our parents to be a part of our life's most important decision. It might have taken weeks or months to win Ananya's parent's trust, but we decided to not lose hope and wait until they agree.

After making many efforts, they agreed, but on one condition that we would get married as soon as possible. Ananya and I were the happiest couple on this planet and got busy with the wedding preparations.

Chapter 26–
The wedding preparations

❄ ❄ ❄

Within a few weeks, we got engaged and fixed December 25 as our wedding date.

It was only three months away.

"We will no longer be boyfriend and girlfriend," I said to Ananya.

She kicked my leg under the table.

"Are you leaving me," she asked angrily.

"No darling, I mean, soon we will become husband and wife," I corrected my statement.

She gave me a loving smile and kissed on my cheeks. We ordered our favorite coffee and discussed our shopping list and our wedding plans.

After a thorough discussion, we prepared a long list of items we were supposed to buy. We prepared a checklist, which contained all the things.

We decided to hire a wedding planner to take care of other arrangements for timely execution of all the events without any interruption, such as venue for engagement, tilak, ladies sangeet, wedding and reception, catering, decoration, photographers, videographer, accommodation for outstation guests and all other necessary provisions.

Ananya was very happy and seeing her smile made me happy to the core.

****

We met regularly in between our busy office schedule and went for shopping.

Apart from buying from local markets, we also visited nearby cities like Jalandhar, Jaipur, Banaras and

Lucknow for shopping.

Our parents were busy in distributing invitation cards. Within two months, we arranged almost everything. Only a month was left for the most awaited day of our life.

Chapter 27–
A Busy Day

❄ ❄ ❄

It was a busy day in my office. I had to finish all my pending work before going for a long leave for my wedding. It was like a daydream. I had to attend many client meetings during the day. I also did not get time to call Ananya. After I got free, I tried her number, but it was not reachable. I called repeatedly, but got the same prompt message. I got worried and called her dad.

"Hello," a slow voice came from the other side of the phone.

"Hello Uncle," I replied while trying to control my emotions.

"Aditya, How are you?" he asked in a gentle tone.

"I am good uncle."

Before he could ask me something, I immediately asked him about Ananya.

"Uncle, may I speak to Ananya as her phone is not reachable."

I had a long conversation with him and what he told made me more worried about her.

He informed me that there was communal violence in Muzaffarnagar and Ananya had left for Muzaffarnagar with her team for ground reporting. Since then her number was not reachable as it was a remote area. I was numb for a few seconds after listening to what Ananya's father informed me.

I was worried about Ananya and could hardly sleep at night.

Chapter 28– A long wait

❄ ❄ ❄

The next day I took off from office despite having a lot of pending work. I switched on the TV early morning to know the news about the riot-hit Muzaffarnagar and to see Ananya reporting from there. This also reminded me of the days when I used to watch TV only to have a glimpse of her.

I had no contact with Ananya since last 24 hours. Every passing minute made me more worried.

I could see the ground reporting on TV. The riots in Muzaffarnagar were between Hindus and Muslims. In India, political parties try to take advantage of such incidents for vote bank.

India is the largest software exporter in the world and we are heading to become a developed nation,

but we are still stuck in the problems related to religion and castes.

****

During the last 24 hours, 20 people were killed, and public property worth crores was set ablaze. Two police officers were also killed. The government gave orders for the deployment of the Army in the affected area as the violence was spreading like fire. Groups of anti-nationalists also took advantages. They misguided people.

I was watching TV, the entire day, and still could not see Ananya reporting.

I tried to call on her number again, but she was still out of reach. I called Ananya's father, but he also did not get any call from her. He had no problem with it. He told me that she was doing her job with her team. He told me not to worry.

I tried to calm myself, but with each passing minute, I got more worried about her.

I was tired and fell asleep. After a few minutes, my phone rang. I opened my eyes and it was Ananya's call.

I picked up the call.

"Hello Adi," a sweet voice came from the other side.

"Hi baby, where are you? I had been trying your number since so long, but it was unreachable," I said.

"Are you crying?" she asked.

"No," I said, though my eyes were filled with water.

"You are lying to me," she said angrily.

"My love I was worried. I tried to contact you, but I was helpless."

"I am fine."

"Your father told me that you went with your team to the riot-hit Muzaffarnagar."

"Yes, my team is here to verify the facts behind the violence and the people behind it," she said.

"But at least you should have informed me before going there."

"Adi everything was planned too quickly that I had no time to inform anyone and I am sorry for that."

"If you had told me about it before, I wouldn't have allowed you to go there. Please come back soon."

"Don't worry Adi, I am fine with my team. I will

come as soon my work gets done."

"I miss you with all my heart. Please come soon."

"Miss you too."

"I love you."

"I love you too."

We hung up the phone.

Chapter 29–
Uncountable Minutes

* * *

I was helpless, and all I could do was only to wait for her to come back. It had been more than two days, since I last met her.

Two more days passed and Ananya's number was still not reachable and even she did not call me.

The situation near the affected region turned fiercer. More than 100 lives were lost. A few reports revealed that a few women were also raped. It is our society's harsh reality that here everything is costly except humanity.

****

It was a dark night. Everything was quiet. It seemed as if silence wanted to whisper something to me. I was in my room watching news.

There was breaking news that flashed on the TV screen that Xpress news channel van was attacked. Two journalists were seriously injured. I panicked and worried about Ananya.

They did not reveal the name of the reporters hurt. I called up at Ananya's office, but no one picked the call. I called Ananya's father and some of her friends, but did not find any information about her.

Finally, I rushed to her office. I came to know that the video journalist, Navneet and Ananya were seriously injured. Ananya was unconscious. They were rushed to hospital by the rescue team.

Sometimes your sixth sense gives you hints that something good or bad is going to happen.

I should have forced Ananya to come back

immediately, but I did not, I cursed myself.

Chapter 30–
The Hospital

❄ ❄ ❄

Medanta Hospital
New Delhi

Ananya was admitted to the ICU. She had several head injuries. An iron rod was used to hit her. There was nothing left in her unconscious body, except that she was alive.

I was sitting outside the ICU and was reading our old conversations. I was recalling our good times and smiled while reading her messages. I was engrossed in my reading when someone called my name.

That was Ananya's father. I immediately hugged him. I wanted to cry, but I controlled my emotions. I consoled him.

We were waiting outside the ICU. A doctor came out of the ICU and told us that due to heavy injury on her skull she was in coma.

"It might take a few hours or a few days or may be a few months for her to gain consciousness. We are doing our best to save her life," said the doctor.

****

Two days passed, but still there was no improvement in Ananya's condition.

Ananya taught me that 'Don't lose hope. It does not matter how difficult the situation is. It would pass with time. Always wear smile on your face. It helps us to fight against all odds.'

After one week:

Ananya was out of danger. However, destiny had decided something else for us.

She suffered a paralytic attack.

Doctor advised that she would take 6 months to 12 months to regain skill, confidence and security in walking.

She could not respond to any of my actions. However, I could see in her eyes that she wanted to talk to me. I spoke to her the whole day, but she did not respond.

She lost sensation in her muscles and could not move her body parts.

She was the most talkative person, but today she was silent.

She was the girl who had always supported me, but today she needed my support.

"Everything will be fine soon," I consoled myself.

Chapter 31
The New Beginning

* * *

After one month

Ananya was discharged from the hospital.

The process of paralysis recovery included proper treatment, spontaneous recovery, and rehabilitation program.

I took her to hospital for daily exercises.

I helped her to get dressed up and eat. Whenever she wanted to move, I would help her as it was to be done carefully because it was very important that all the limbs be in the correct posture.

It became my routine.

After three months

Now her condition was getting better. A few of her body parts started moving.

Occasionally, I took her to the same coffee house where we first met.

I believed in my love and that one day she would be perfectly fine. We would get married soon and fulfill our dreams together.

I cried a little by holding her hands and promised her that I would never leave her. Because, It happens only in love.

****The End****

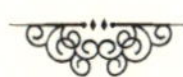

Epilogue:

❄ ❄ ❄

I wish I had the superpower to unfold the pages of future so that I could know what is good and what is bad that would happen in my life. . I would never be the same person if Ananya didn't came into my life.

We moved to Kerala for a few months for her Ayurvedic treatment. Ananya had a slow recovery. She endured few painful therapies. She started speaking but was still unable to walk. At one point, I was told she may never walk again but I am determined not give up on her. There is no ending until it's a happy one. Now, we go on long walks while she is on her wheel chair. She talks nonstop just like she used to do before. She gave me new essence of love. "Love can make us, Love can break us. We must learn how to deal with it."

About the Author

* * *

Amit Singh hails from Lucknow. He is a computer science graduate. Lives in New Delhi and is currently working with DXC Technology, Noida. He is very fond of reading novels, loves to play guitar and travels in his spare time. He has a poetic heart and loves to write poems and stories.

You can know more about him:
Facebook- fb.me/writeramitsingh
Twitter - https://twitter.com/writeramit29
Instagram-@writeramit29
Or write to him at - writeramit29@gmail.com